Scorpion Tales

First published in Australia in 2018

Normoyle and Cogan Bespoke *Publishers*

ABN 55 250 263 315

www.normoyleandcoganpublishers.com

A catalogue record for this book is available from the National Library of Australia.

ISBN 978-0-6484002-2-6 (paperback)

ISBN 978-0-6484002-3-3 (ebook)

Cover design by Donna Dean

Typeset Georgia and Times New Roman by Siobhan Colman

Printed and bound by Lightning Source Australia

Acting is standing up naked and turning
around very slowly.

Rosalind Russell

When you can't wait for your ship to come in,
you've got to row out to it.

Greer Garson

The great gift of human beings is that we have
the power of empathy.

Meryl Streep

For those with no voice.

Scorpion Tales

Siobhan Colman

Scorpion Tales

Final Call

Business Class Lounge at airport.

WOMAN. Early thirties. Smartly dressed in a business suit.

WOMAN

(Finishing the last of her glass of champagne and pouring herself another.)

He wraps me in golden warmth. Like the blanket Grandma had on my bed when I was little – when she'd tuck me in and tell me the angels would watch over me. I can't remember what colour it was. Just the way it felt.

He's like that. My body relaxes when I hear his voice. I feel safe.

I am safe with him.

(Pause.)

And I'll be ok.

(Long pause. She sips her drink.)

I've made such a mess of things. All my relationships have been a series of derailments leading to the final twisted wreck. I can't help myself *(smiles sadly)*. I have a thing for control freaks. This last one was a wolf in sheep's clothing. *(Rubs face as though the bruises still show.)*

I count myself lucky to have walked away with some pride and dignity. At least on the outside. *(Pause.)*

Inside there was a weeping wound and a

screaming child.

I'd given up believing there would be a rescue.

Until now.

(Pause. Raises glass to look at the bubbles and wipe away the frosting.)

I'm not a religious person. At least I wasn't for a long time. After my Grandma had her stroke all talk of angels stopped with her tongue. And DoCS came in and had me removed.

No more blankets.

They didn't let me visit. "Too distressing," they said.

It's amazing how deaf people can be to the sound of screaming. It's like cicadas in summer. You hear the first one but when they are calling in their thousands, you tune the noise out. Now, the only way you'll notice them is when they stop. It's amazing how loud silence can be.

(Pause.)

She didn't last long after that. And I waited. I waited until I had the chance to join her.

(Smiles at audience.)

Oh. It's not all doom and gloom. We rise above things.

He taught me that.

(Sips drink and pours more.)

He had waited too. Let me find my own way to him. Had shown me the door was open, had let me see inside him.

He's taken nothing from me. Only given.

He's light. And I'm trembling in that light. *(Closes eyes with relief.)*

He is heat and safety. A fire-place on a winter's night.

(Long pause.)

I wasn't a wife. Or a girlfriend, though I had friends who hoped I'd find the right man.

(Pause.)

And I wasn't miserable, either. I'd found a strange kind of contentment in being alone. It served my purpose.

(Holds up bottle to examine how much is left. Takes a long swallow from her glass and pours more.)

I met him online.

(Smiles.)

I wasn't looking.

I'd never even heard of them, but one day there

was a curious message in my inbox:

The Solution: Be a part of it.

He's a part of it.

(Smiles nervously. Looks at watch and begins to collect her travel documents while speaking.)

And here I am. Two years later – with my passport and my ticket.

I haven't bothered with a suitcase. I'm not coming back.

(Checks her purse.)

The small powder compact in my purse is enough. They will detonate it from the ground.

And I'll head into the next life. See my Grandma. Be protected by angels.

"It will be instant," he told me. "You won't need to do anything but get on board. I have bought you a business class seat. Only the best for you.”

He told me to drink as much as they offered and then take the sleeping tablet.

I’ll be asleep when it happens.

(Stands to leave. Takes out her phone.)

I’ve written my manifesto. I’ll send it to the *Times* just before the plane takes off. It’s a late flight on a long weekend and the journalists will be out till Tuesday.

By the time anyone reads it it will all be over.

CALL TO BOARD FLIGHT

He loves me.

His love is the purest of all. Not of this world *(takes a final swig of champagne)* but of the next.

END

The Priest

DEIRDRE: Seventeen from Crocke, a tiny village in County Limerick. It is 1963. She's dressed as though it's still the '50's, but she's tried to style her hair in the latest beehive. She's at the kitchen sink.

DEIRDRE

Sean's gone up to Dublin. Left this morning. Mammy's so proud of him. And he looked so neat and tidy in his suit.

He's always been neat and tidy. Not like my other brothers. They're always covered in muck from the cowshed, or the soccer field. They bash down the kitchen door with their huge selves, throw their boots about the place and wolf down the whole loaf saved for dinner. Mammy never minds their smell, or their loud voices. And for a while she didn't say anything when they tied Sean up in the hay barn, or stole his school books, or called him names. Sean doesn't play football. And he isn't loud. His voice is high and soft – like mine. And he plays the piano.

Sometimes he plays so I cry. Sean can play all my hidden thoughts, though I've never talked to him about them. "I can see 'em, Deidre. Ye can't hide much from me."

When we were little, Sean and I took to playing in Mammy's room. I was playing with her dressing table – smelling all the perfumes and powders. When I looked up in the mirror I saw Sean. Reflected. Standing in front of the wardrobe. He was wearing Mammy's dress and shoes. I watched as he straightened the skirt, just like Mammy, how he fixed the flowerets at the collar.

'Sean!' I could not find any words. I wanted to tell him he looked better in that dress than Mammy. That he was beautiful. That it looked the most natural thing in the world. That I'd never seen him look stronger. But I said nothing. Just his name.

And then Mammy came through the door.

She stood frozen when she saw him. Her face an ashen white. I remember thinking that she looked like she'd covered her cheeks in powder because their rosiness had gone.

"What do ye think ye're doing?" She was looking at him. Her hand had gone to the cupboard to steady herself. "Sean?"

My brother took a deep breath and smoothed his

fingers over the fabric. Then he opened his mouth. "Practicing for the priesthood, Mammy. I'm wearing the robes."

"The priesthood?" Mammy blinked.

I shot Sean a look, amazed. We both knew he was lying. I felt my heart swell with admiration.

Colour was returning to Mammy's cheeks. "The priesthood, you say." She wiped her face with the hanky she always kept in her apron pocket. "Well, Sean. That's grand! It's something I've always hoped for one of my boys." She was smiling now. "'Tis a grand thing!"

From then on Sean often wore Mammy's clothes. But not when the boys were home. And I watched him, fascinated. Even when I was older, I never looked in my own clothes as good as Sean looked in Mammy's.

And then Sean went away to the Brothers and was only home on holidays. And I missed him. Sometimes so much I felt my heart would burst. And then he found a special friend in Jimmy Gill. They would hide away in the cow shed for hours and I was not allowed in.

But I liked Jimmy. He brought me presents and wove me daisy chains and he always wore a pink scarf with a blue stripe. And when I watched them together I remembered that first day in Mammy's room when he wore her dress.

One day when Sean was up the road delivering Mammy's soup to old Mrs O'Rouke, Jimmy arrived at our back door. His eye was swollen and his nose was bleeding. Mammy brought him into the kitchen. She didn't say anything to him, just wrapped her great warm arms around him. And he cried. I was frightened. Jimmy Gill was seventeen.

His pink scarf was missing and there was a bloody mark on the back of his trousers. I took a rug from the chair and wrapped it around him. So as no one could see. But he didn't stop crying.

When Sean came home and saw him Sean looked like someone had shot him. He looked like that for a long time.

They both left this morning. Sean and Jimmy. And Mammy dreams of her son a priest. "'Tis a fast track into heaven," Mammy smiles. "Though it will have its trials, no doubt."

I look at her and nod. I don't have the heart to tell her Sean will never be a priest. Bless him.

There are no words.

END

The Cow

RACHEL sits in the driver's seat of a car, facing the audience.

RACHEL

It comes out of nowhere. The cow. Right there in the middle of the freeway – on the other side of the road. It's bellowing. Frozen as the oncoming traffic swerves around it. I try not to look. Any moment it will be hit and killed. Any moment. No-one is stopping for it. No-one is gently leading it away to safety. And I can't cross the road to save it.

It would be suicide.

As I pass it I turn my rear view mirror so I can't see it reflected there on the road. And my hand reaches for the volume on the radio. Anything but hear it screaming. I don't want to hear the inevitable....

(Pause.)

My hands are shaking long after I exit the freeway. So much so I have to pull off the road. It's a safe neighbourhood. Comfortable houses and manicured lawns. Much like my own neighbourhood. Clean lines and picket fences.

I want to be sick. I'm too shaken to keep driving. I'll just sit here a few moments. I know I can't be late home. My husband doesn't like it.

In my head I can still hear the mournful wailing of that cow. 'Rachel! Rachel!' it's howling. Like a dog on a choker chain. 'Rachel!' My name.

I manage to get the car door open before I'm sick all over the road.

(Pause.)

It's a few minutes before I realise I'm being watched. Across the street the house seems empty, but the curtain has just moved. A slow, careful movement so as to appear no-one is there. A deliberate, slow nudging of curtain.

A chill crawls up my spine. Somebody's there. I know it. I can hear my mother (*Irish accent*) 'Someone's walked over my grave, Rachel!' She said it often when I was young until she was in the grave herself. Life took a sharp turn south when she died.

Then I hear it. Her voice. Not in my memory but here, in this street, somewhere outside the car. I look to the house and see a hand. It's moving the curtain to reveal the darkness behind it. But I can't see anyone. They won't show their face.

'Rachel!' says my mother. 'Rachel! Run!'

I need to get home. Dinner's at six. My husband will be waiting and if there's no dinner on the table he'll... There's steak in the boot. The best cut. I tried giving him mince once. I made a lovely meat loaf – my mother's recipe, her special spices and that drop of brandy which made it so moist. I thought he'd love it. I dressed up nicely. I even put on lipstick and that perfume he told me to wear. I was at the door when he got home. The house was tidy and I made sure dinner was on the table.

'What's this?' he stared at it.

'Meatloaf. Mum's meatloaf.'
His eyes narrowed and he picked up the plate, and

I could smell it: that wonderful savoury aroma, straight from the oven.

He sniffed at it. 'Dog food,' he said. 'If you think I'll eat this shit then you're crazy.' He spat the words at me.

'But if you'll just taste it!' I should have kept my mouth shut.

'Dogs eat dog food.' He hissed and grabbed my hair. 'Here,' he pushed my face into the plate. 'Eat, dog!' I struggled to get loose, but he was angry now. He pushed me to the floor and took off his belt.

(Long pause.)

He's not a bad man. He's just stressed at work. And I brought it on myself. He works so hard that he needs things just right when he gets home. I wasn't thinking.

(Peers in the direction of the house.)

Someone's there. I know it. Watching. *(shivers)* 'Someone's just walked over my grave, Mum.'

(Pause.)

I don't want to tell him I'm pregnant. I didn't think I could ever have a child after that night he'd been drinking. The next morning he slept in and I took myself to the medical centre. They said I needed stitches. That I really should take myself to emergency. The nurse looked at me with pity. I left as soon as they were through. Couldn't spare the time for pain killers. Needed to be home before he knew I was gone. Had to manage on Panadol.

(Rubs belly.)

Soon it will be obvious.

(Pause.)

My mother used to sing me lullabies. Beautiful Irish songs her mother sang to her.

(sings)

Toora- loora-loora,

Toora-loora-lie,

Toora-loora-loora,

Hush now, don't you cry

(repeats, but can't finish. Is quietly weeping.)

It's me, isn't it Mum. That cow on the freeway. It's me! And no-one is stopping to help. No-one is slowing down. No-one is leading me to safety. And I'm screaming! I'm screaming!

Everyone can see it. I know they think I should leave, that there are places to go, but they don't understand. And they're watching. Pitying. Shaking their faceless heads. Their empty, faceless concern behind chinks in curtains. Something dark is coming and they watch behind glass. Turn up their radios to smother the sound of this cow screaming.

And I can't move. I can't move! I'm smothering in my own terror but I can't cross the road.

(Long pause. Looks at watch.)

It's after six. He'll be home. Waiting.

(Long pause. Starts engine.)

He's not a bad man.

END

The Elephant

DEEDEE: 7 years old. Playing on swing equipment in backyard. Plays, poses, stretches, chews gum etc. throughout.

DEEDEE

Harry can't come out to play any more. Mum keeps him inside. In his bedroom. 'Was he bad?' I asked her.

Boys can be bad. They can't help it though. It's what they're made of. If I was made of slugs and snails I think I'd be rotten.

But it might be fun.

Harry builds things. He's good at it. Any spare bits of glue and paper, sticks and nails bits of wire. He can build anything. He built me an elephant once. Not a real one, silly. But it looked real. It was this big *(stretches out arms as far as they will go)* and I could sit on it. He made it outta paper and a glue Mum boiled on the stove. It took him a week, but when it was finished it was perfect.

"That's too big to bring indoors," said Mum. "It won't fit through the back door." So I got to sit on it in the garden and play Tarzan in the Jungle and Harry was my monkey. It lasted for ages. Until it rained.

Harry has a sling shot. *(Covers mouth in shock as she realises she's giving away secrets.)* Don't tell Mum! He keeps it under the wood pile in the corner near the pool *(points)*.

Oh, I forgot. We don't have a pool now. Daddy took it down. It took him a whole day and I watched him through the back door. I wasn't allowed outside. And it must have been a lot of work because he was crying as he drained the water. I understand. I cry sometimes when I have too much work.

I hate work. Mum gives me chores to do and lately she's been giving me Harry's chores too. Like raking the garden and dragging out the Otto bin. 'How come he's not having to do it?" I ask her, but it only makes her angry. Well, not angry. I don't know what it makes her. And I feel a bit... strange when she's like that. So now I don't say anything. I just do Harry's chores, *(takes small note book from pocket)* but I'm marking it down in this book. And I'm gonna make sure that, as soon as Harry can come outside, he will have to do my chores for a while.

I'm glad the pool's gone 'cause cleaning it was one of his chores. He liked to use the 'Creepy Crawly' and tinker with the filter. I asked him 'How does the Creepy Crawley know which bits of the pool to clean?' He laughed at me. "It doesn't. It's random." I nodded, but I don't know what random is. Maybe it's like magic. But I didn't ask him. I want him to think I'm smart like him. And I want to make things like he does. 'Cause he's made loads more than an elephant and a sling shot.

'Whatcha need the sling shot for?' I asked him when he showed me.

"Protection," he said.

'Whatcha need protection for?'

"Not for me, you numbskull. For Bluey. For next

time Bluey's dad blacks his mum's eye."

Bluey is Harry's best friend. He's littler than Harry. He's kinda the same size as me. And he laughs a lot. And he used to spend heaps of time here in our backyard 'cause his back yard is full of old tyres and bent bits of iron and dog poo and garbage. I only saw it once when we walked him home. But I've never really met his mum. She didn't come out of her room, though she said hello through the door. She sounded nice.

Bluey's always at our place – helping Harry with his inventions. And he's ok with Mum. But when Dad is home he seems a bit nervous. So Dad tries really hard to make his time here fun.

I haven't seen Bluey since Harry's been kept indoors. The two of them must have done something really bad. Badder than bad. But Mum won't tell me what it is and Dad hasn't been in a good mood since the pool. Maybe he hurt himself on the sharp metal sides, or on the ladder when he was pulling it down. 'Cause I've seen him crying – even when there's no work to do.

I'm not allowed in Harry's room. They've locked the door. And he won't answer me when I whisper at the lock. 'Whatcha do? Harry, how come they're so mad at you? Harry? Harry? If you don't answer me, I'll tell Bluey you wear pink underpants!' But he won't answer me. He must be trying to be good.

Now I just slip notes under the door and wait for replies. Nothing so far.

I'm not really worried. School starts next week and he's going into Year Seven. I'm going into Year Three. They'll let him out for school for sure.

And I'm not so bored. We've had loads of visitors.
First the electrician – because something was
wrong with our electricity. He spent ages looking
at the pool filter and the chord leading from the
house. And we've had Grandma and Grandpa over.
And now there's a man with a black shirt and a
little white patch on his collar and Mum is making
him some tea. And yesterday two women arrived
in white suits with hats and they showed Mum and
Dad some pictures and they sent me outside to
play.

Harry's not bad. He's better than anyone I know.

END

Penance

WOMAN in her mid-forties.

She is busy tidying her living room, dusting and cleaning while speaking.

WOMAN

I want everything to be just right. I want him to see I'm alright. To see I've sorted myself out.

(Picks up photo of young woman.)

This is Carol. She's off at university now. I made sure I did everything I could to give her a chance. Worked nights after I put her to bed. Did that for years after.... Until she was old enough to realise. Such a wise kid, she was. 'It's Ok, Mum. I want to go to the local public school. I don't want to go anywhere else. I'll be ok. You need to be home." She was eleven years old, but she was wiser than me.

I'd gone to a good school. St Ashmore Lady's College. And even though I wasn't top of the grade, I was doing all right. I had good friends and I liked the teachers. Mostly. I didn't even mind the prayers and the masses and the bells.

He went to the boys' school. St Francis. And I liked him. Had liked him for ages. I would see him from the bus in his soccer shorts and t-shirt. Even in winter. He seemed like a god then.

(Pause.)

When he asked me to dance with him I felt like I'd

won the lottery.

(Pause.)

But the way he touched me made me feel... dirty.

(Pause.)

I shouldn't have gone outside the hall with him. I should have gone straight home with my friends. It still amazes me – the steep price of one poor decision.

(Long pause. Folds duster distractedly.)

It wasn't rape. I fancied myself in love with him. But I know now that he took something from me that night that I can't get back. He took something. And he gave me something.

John knew. It took me years to find a good man. But he was a good man. And when we had Carol life was close to perfect. John used to wake in the night when she woke crying and I'd see him dancing with her, waltzing around the bedroom with rapture on his face and her little hand tugging at his beard. I'd leave them to it: that tiny moment of unquestioning love and care. And I remember thinking to myself that things can't get any better. But I was terrified, too, that something might happen to take it all away.

John was a rigger. One of those jolly, burley, blokey blokes who whistles their way through life. Hard work, good pay, long hours. He was gone before dawn and home just as I was putting her to bed.

(Pause.)

I don't remember that last morning. Not his bristly kiss, or the bang of the screen door. The grumble of his ute as he revved it in the drive. Safe sounds.

Sounds so safe they had become part of the background (*voice catches*). He'd become part of my background.

(Long pause.)

I didn't believe them at first. The Police. I'd seen it all so many times in the movies. That knock at the door, that visit with maudlin faces. This was a young police woman and an even younger male constable. They were sweating through their uniforms. And as the words registered: 'crane… powerline… died instantly…' all I remember is those dark blue stains, spreading like ink on blotting paper on their light blue shirts. "So sorry," they were saying. "Is there anyone we can call? Your mother?"

No.

(Long pause.)

My mother told me it would be for the best. Twenty five years ago. I could finish school. *(Mother's voice.)* "No-one needs to know. It'll be better off with someone who can care for it. Better off. We can send you to my sister's. We'll tell the neighbours you've gone on exchange to Japan. Too late for an abortion. Should have told me sooner. But still, there are ways and means. Ways and means."

I was sent away to stay with my cousins until it was time to have the baby. Like someone with a disease. Mum arranged everything. She knew people. I signed the papers after they'd given me the pethidine. It was all a blur.

But when he was born I remember the smell of him. Warm, soft and wet from the birth. And I remember his great swathe of hair, thick and brown. Like the boy from St Francis. And I remember his scream and his struggle as the nurses wrapped him in blankets and took him away.

Punishment for my sin. Penance. I am branded here, *(rubs forehead as though making a 'sign of the cross' in the 'Glory Be' in mass)* and here, *(rubs eyes)* and here, *(rubs heart)* here there is a slow bleed.

(Long pause.)

Carol doesn't know she has a brother. I will see how this afternoon goes before I tell her.

What if he's disappointed? He asked very little on the phone. Just enough to know he'd found me. I was so shocked I can't remember what I said except Yes. Yes. Come when you're ready.

(Pause.)

I want to tell him I'm sorry. I want to tell him that

never once forgot him. That I tried to find him, just after John died, but they wouldn't give me his new name.

(Pause.)

I couldn't look at my own mother after they took him. And I dropped out of school. My friends had found other friends in the months I was away. They didn't take too kindly to secrets. And I couldn't talk to them. I'd stopped trying. That light inside me had been snuffed out.

SOUND OF DOORBELL.

He's here.

(Puts away her cleaning things. Looks at herself in the mirror.)

DOOR BELL RINGS TWICE IN QUICK SUCCESSION.

(Smiles.) He must be nervous.

(Calls out beyond the door.) On my way!

(Picks up Carol's photo. Rubs it fondly. Decisively. Straightens her dress and runs a hand through her hair. There is a strength and youthfulness in her step as she heads for the door)

On my way.

END

The Sandwich

PHIL, a man in his thirties. In a wheelchair in a kitchen. He is busy making sandwiches.

PHIL

(Cuts bread while speaking.)

She'll eat this. It's funny how everything else is gone, but she can still eat a sandwich. She'll sit like a little girl in a milk bar with her legs swinging and her whole concentration on the white-bread triangles between her fingers. Like the first day I saw her when we were kids.

(Cleans crumbs from the bench and puts them in the bin.)

She used to be such a clean freak. Nothing to be left on the bench, wash the kitchen floor after every meal. Even after breakfast. Drove me mad. Drove us all mad.

We should have known then. It got worse. So bad the kids would cringe when she came in the door.

I didn't realise. Not in the beginning. Not even when I knew something was wrong. And for a while I thought she was just extra snappy, extra callous. Thought something must have happened at work.

(Butters each piece of bread slowly while speaking.)

The kids didn't tell me. Bless them. But how could they tell me they thought their mother was mad?

So they made the best of their time before she came home. And they pretended everything was fine, even when it all began unravelling. Even when she threw things. Even when she screamed long and loud like a banshee – a chilling, unearthly sound.

When it first happened it brought the neighbours through our back door.

"Phil! Phil, are you ok?" They found me in my wheelchair covered in flour. "We thought you musta died or something!" She was talking to the fridge. And the kids – the kids were sitting frozen at the kitchen table pretending the neighbours had not seen anything unusual. She'd grabbed a packet of flour and hurled it like it had burned her fingers.

I knew then that something was wrong with my

wife.

(Opens a tin of tuna and puts it in a bowl while speaking.)

I was home and took the call when her work phoned. She'd been let go. They had no choice. She'd threatened the manager with the jagged lid from a baked bean tin. No. They didn't call the police. No, they didn't think she had calmed down before she left – they had shut her in the store room and called Human Resources. But she was gone when they opened the door. She had climbed out the window. Like a criminal. But she had defecated. She'd defecated on the photocopy paper and smeared some of it on the wall. "It'll have to come out of her pay," they said. "Her last pay."

"Sometimes these things are treatable," her specialist said when we got her to the hospital.

"Unfortunately, hers is not. And it's growing faster than we'd expect. Has she been behaving erratically?"

I nodded. And I confess I found his question darkly funny. 'She put the cat in the dryer yesterday – is that erratic enough?' It had been ok. My eldest has taken it upon herself to monitor her mother. At a safe distance. Pudding was released alive and disgruntled. We've sent him to live with friends.

"The nerves," said the specialist. "The thing is pressing on several areas of the brain. She may suffer migraines. She may become docile. But this area," he pointed to the scan of my wife's brain. Great dark shadows stretched across it like the images in my father's school books of communism during the cold war. "This area may cause her agitation and paranoia. And some patients become violent."

(Opens a jar of mayonnaise and spoons it into a bowl. Adds spices while talking.)

'Any chance she'll recover?'

"No. We're trialling several treatments, but I don't think she's suitable for any."

'How long does she have?'

"It's hard to say."

'Weeks?'

He laughed at this. "Oh, no, my dear fellow. Most likely years."

She knows. In those moments when she's ok and she's her old self, she'll laugh, or move to tickle the kids. But they flinch. And the look. The look in her eyes. Like some great open pit of sadness. Black and engulfing. I have to wheel myself to the kitchen then. Tell her I'm making us all a hot chocolate. She nods like a lost little girl. Bewildered, but aware the forest is in shadows and night is falling.

"Help me!" she whispered one night as we lay together. She had crept under my arm like she did when we were first married. Her head on my chest. Her soft hair falling about her face, covering her eyes like a golden veil.

"Help me," she whispered. "Help me go before I'm gone!"

My breath caught. I hadn't expected her to say it. But I found myself nodding and combing her hair. Her jasmine-scented hair. 'It will be all right.'

She was crying now, so softly. "If you love me you'll help me go."

'Shh,' I say. 'I love you enough.'

(Pause.)

She sighs then. A great long breath of relief. And she sleeps.

(Pause.)

I have not slept properly since.

(Takes out a packet of pills. Opens it. Pops the pills in a cup and slowly crushes them with a spoon.)

Little bundles of pain relief. Opiate. For my shattered spine. It's been a while since I've taken any. I had to have enough. And the chemists are observant. Medications are precise. It's taken months to be sure of the amount.

(Takes jar out of the cupboard. It is full of white powder.)

She hasn't been herself for over a month. Her only

peace is after dinner for an hour or so before the screaming starts.

(Adds the mayonnaise to the tuna in a bowl. Slowly adds the white powder from the jar and the cup. Stirs purposefully. Makes the sandwiches. Cuts them into triangles. Takes out some rocket leaves. Adds the rocket)

Tandoori and lime mayonnaise are fabulous with tuna. Hide a multitude of sins. She'll notice the bitterness so I'll add some rocket. She'll eat it. And for an hour, or two, she'll sit quietly.

(Pause.)

She is my life.

(Pause.)

It will take a while.

I'll put on a movie and we'll sit together as a

family.

(Puts sandwiches on a tray. Places the tray gently on his lap. Stares down at it for a moment lost in thought. We see a flicker of fear, followed by resignation before his gaze finds the audience.)

One last time.

END

The Book

Woman in her thirties, MYRIAM. Wearing hijab. Modestly dressed. At kitchen table folding nappies. There is an open door a few feet away leading off stage where we can hear happy, child-like sounds (Esha).

MYRIAM

(References child off stage.)

Esha is my youngest. She has two older sisters. My husband wanted a son. Even though I was not young, he said it was his right. To have a son. Someone to carry the name.

Sons are gods in the old country.

Daughters are …

My Eldest, Resa, she is my heart. She is seventeen now. She is very good at school. Yesterday she is voted Vice Captain. I am so happy when she comes home to tell me. "You are like Rabia Basri, the prophet, I tell her. A blessing on us! I will make you a special meal!"

It's Ramadan and a time of fasting, but I do not think Allah will mind. We fast until sunset. But last night we feast!

She has nine months more of school. Her grades are good. She is smart. She wishes to go to university. She will be the first woman of my family to go to university.

My husband wishes her to marry.

He does not believe she should go to university.

(In her husband's voice.) "Her husband will

provide. She must do as Allah commands: serve her husband. Give him children. Give *me* grandchildren. Grandsons!"

When he says these things she looks to the floor. I see colour in her cheeks. She holds her breath. Her fists are pale from clenching them tight. But she says nothing. What can she say? In our culture a daughter must obey her father.

A wife must obey her husband.

It has always been this way.

Tima is my second child. This year she has begun high school. Her grades are not good. Always she asks " Why?" to her teachers.

(In Tima's voice.) "Why must I study history? No-one ever learns from it. Why must I wear a uniform? I learn better in jeans. Why must I follow

rules? Some rules kill people…"

Last week they call me to the school. Tima has walked out of her class. Scripture. She has been disrespectful. "God does not exist!"

I thank Allah that my husband was at work. He would have beaten her. Not for walking out of the class. For her words.

She does not walk home. They find her in the library, on the floor. She has a book in her hands. They tell me she will not leave until she borrows the book. They try and try, but still she will not move. They do not want her to have the book. "Why?" I ask them. "It is a library. Is it not a place for books?"

They tell me she borrows a reference book. For teachers. Not for students.

"What is this book?" I ask.

They show me.

(Long pause.)

I have seen this book, once, when I was only a girl.

It was banned in my country.

But my aunty, she finds this book in the hotel where she cleans. It is in English. She does not speak the language, but she keeps the book. She shows the women of my family and we wonder at it and fear it. Like a dark secret. Until her husband finds it hidden in a cupboard.

He reports her to the authorities.

And they beat her for blasphemy. In front of her children, her family. The village comes to watch.

They burn the book. But I remember the name.

And the cover. I will always remember the name.

The Female Eunuch.

(Long pause. Nervously folding and refolding nappies.)

I am afraid for my daughter.

My husband does not love her. He frowns to look at her.

"A daughter must respect her father," I tell her gently when she cries. She nods when I say this. Then she looks at me, her eyes dark with sorrow.

"But I cannot."

My husband says she must leave school when she is sixteen. "Fatima must marry before men know she is defiant!"

I say to him "She must say at school until she is eighteen. It is the law here."

He looks at me, his fist clenched as though he will hit me. But he does not. Instead his eyes flash with

something I do not trust. (*In husband's voice.*)
"Then we will go some place else."

I would leave with my daughters. But I cannot. I have no job. I did not finish school. And my English is poor.

And Esha, my beautiful Esha, needs care. Her birth was long. The doctors tell me something is not right. They tell me there is no oxygen.

When she comes she is blue. Blue! I have never seen skin that colour. She is struggling. She is not crying. But she is alive.

And I know she is a gift from Allah which I must learn to open.

My husband does not look at her.

He says we will give her away, but I tell him the government will pay us to keep her.

"Kafirs!" he laughs. "Fools! You must hide her from my family. I will tell them she is dead. It is better."

When he is not home we are happy. Resa and Tima, they help me care for Esha. She laughs to see her sisters. She sleeps long in their arms.

I worry what will happen when they are gone. How Esha will grieve. How I will mend my own heart.

(Checks she is alone. Reaches into the bottom of the basket and pulls out a cloth bag. Inside the bag is cash.)

I have some money. I keep it in the basket with the nappies. He will not look here.

I know Resa cannot stay. I must get her away where he cannot find her. She must take Tima with her. There are shelters. Places for them.

I know Resa will take care of her sister.

She must go to university.

This is not the old country. She is free here.

But only if she leaves.

I will tell her "Go! Make a life for yourself and for Tima. When you settle I will bring Esha and we will be happy!"

I will smile. I will give her my best linen and the blanket my mother wove for me when I was a child. She will be warm and her life will be as she chooses.

She is a smart girl.

She will go.

She will take her sister whose spirit is slowly dying here.

She will do as I ask.

If Allah is willing, I will see my daughters again.

We will not speak of what my husband will do when he finds out what I have done. We will not speak of it. I will hide my terror behind a veil. Tell her all will be well.

She will smile to give me strength. She will kiss my cheek and play with Esha's tiny fingers as though today is as yesterday.

And she will go.

END

Transitioning

Teenager (GIRL or BOY). Sitting on a bed in typical adolescent bedroom. Surrounded by books, pens, etc. There is a phone and an open computer on the bed beside them. In their lap is a photo album. They turn pages as they speak.

GIRL/BOY

Dad wasn't always my Dad. Once he was my Mum.

(Pause.)

I haven't told the gang at school. Not yet anyway.

It's not that they wouldn't understand. I think

they'd be pretty cool about it. It's just, well, I'm still working out how I feel about it all. And until I can work that out I won't open my mouth.

When he was Mum she cried a lot. She'd stare into space, tears in her eyes. She'd dye her hair a hundred colours and bring women home for coffee.

But she was soft. Gentle. She spent more time with me than he does now. She would wrap her soft arms around me and cuddle me for hours.

To me she was beautiful. The best mum in the world.

When I look at the old photos now I can see that, as a woman, she was handsome. Strong jaw. Large hands. But so beautiful she could have been a model. And tall. There are pictures of her when I was five and she's wearing a dress. All flowery and flowy. The sun is in her hair and she's staring at the camera like some movie star.

But even then I can see it. The pain. There in her eyes. A piercing look as though she could run away. Or kill herself. Or kill someone else.

By the time I was ten she'd stopped wearing dresses. I didn't really notice at the time. But I can see it now. Just turn the page in the album and they're gone.

Turn a few more pages and *she's* gone.

What I did notice was the things she did. She cut her hair short and began to roll up her sleeves. She kept a pack of cigarettes rolled in one sleeve, matches in the other. And she bought herself weights and began to work out. In the back room. With the blinds drawn. Like a caterpillar shyly pupating within its cocoon.

She stopped bringing anyone home for coffee. She stopped seeing people entirely. She worked from home. IT. For a company which cared so little about her as a person, it gave her so much more freedom to become someone else.

But at the dinner table – and she always said a family must eat together, at the table, and share their day- "A mark of refinement." – she was still Mum; making sure I ate all my pumpkin, taking the gristly meat from my plate, giving me more mashed potato because she knew I liked potato. And we'd talk about our day.

I don't know when I realised that I did all the talking. She listened. Like mothers do. And she took her little pill with her dinner each night, with a glass of carrot juice. When I asked her what the pill was for she smiled and said, "It makes me more myself."

"Do I need to be more myself?" I asked her.

"No. You're perfect as you are."

Change – when it happens to people like her – comes slowly. Gradually. Her deep voice grew deeper, its honey tones fell away to a rasp. Her neck lost its slenderness, her hands grew rough and there were muscles under her rolled-up sleeves. One day I came home from school and noticed there was hair on her face - darker, thicker – not the soft snowy down she'd had before.

By the time I was in Year 7 she'd had a mastectomy. I remember when she came home from the hospital how she winced when I hugged her. But that look in her eyes was gone. She smiled as she showed me the bandages, covered by an oversized men's shirt.

That little pill at dinner continued, but now I knew

what it was. And with it came changes in her
moods.

Once I caught her staring at her face in the
bathroom mirror. At the changes. Her eyes were
now more deeply set, her strong jaw was broad
and square, her complexion was less rosy. Pimples
she'd lost in her teens now returned with a
vengeance. She borrowed my pimple cream.

What did she see when she looked at herself?

What was she looking for?

For a while, when she cuddled me, she let me go
after only a few moments. And I was crushed by
the strength of her. She didn't notice when I stood
ready to tell her about my day as she prepared
dinner. The gristle stayed on my plate and there
were no extra potatoes.

This year she sat me down at the table and talked

to me about pronouns. From now on she was a *he*. It wasn't a shock to me that she said it. But it was shocking just the same.

"But you're my Mum!"

"I was your Mum. But now I'm your Dad."

"But you're not my Dad! He's off somewhere with a new family."

She took a breath. "Yes, I know. You have one Dad, but now you have another."

I felt my eyes tearing up, but I didn't want to cry. "Why? Why do I have to have another? I only had one Mum!"

"I know. But I'm not the same as I was when I had you."

"Really?" I snapped. "Can't tell!"

"Don't be cruel," she said. "I know you know what

I mean. I just need you to begin to come to terms with it. So I want you to try to think of me now as your father. It's who I am now. I'm now your dad."

I broke down hearing this. I just wanted to claw back every moment which had taken my mother away. Every day had been a step away from her.

"I won't!" I said finally, "I won't call you Dad. You're my Mum. You'll always be my Mum. You can't just take that away from me."

(Pause.)

He said nothing. Just looked at me and for the first time in ages I could see tears in his eyes. It was as though he finally understood how much he'd asked. That he'd crossed a line for me that I would never cross.

"Ok," he said after a long silence. "I understand." There was such sadness in his eyes now, where before there had been hope. And for a second I saw that old look of panic and desperation I hadn't seen for years. I felt it in my stomach. Winded. And it scared me.

"If you'll be my Mum at home," I found myself saying, "then maybe I can call you Tom when we're out." My mother had been christened Tomasina. She'd said she hated the name, would change it in a heartbeat.

He brightened at this. "Tom." He repeated it. "Tom - has a nice ring to it. A good, solid name."

He smiled and ruffled my hair. "Deal!"

That night he took the gristle off my meat and gave me extra potato.

Now I get around the whole pronoun thing with *you* and *their* – all a bit cryptic, but really, I've noticed that people accept what you say up front.

If I have to, I'll use *he*.

And I'm beginning to see him as a he. Tom.

In some ways he's like a new friend – one you instantly click with. He knows me and I know him.

We have each other's back.

And maybe, some time soon, I'll tell the gang at school about my mother, Tom.

END

Father's Son

YOUNG FATHER, nineteen years old. Stands in a messy living room. A bag of nappies is strewn all over the floor. There are unwashed plates of food, half eaten, and an ash tray full of cigarette butts. He slowly begins to tidy up as he speaks.

YOUNG FATHER

I didn't mean it. Honest. I'm not like my Dad.

I tell her to get milk for the baby. I tell her to clean up this mess.

Like a proper wife.

Like the kind of mum my own Mum was.

But she sits on her ass in front of the TV. She doesn't even watch it.

She doesn't even hear the baby. She doesn't even clean herself up.

Lately, she'd begun to stink.

And I'm thinking if wasn't for my son I'd leave her. But I can't look after him on my own. I shouldn't have to. It's her job. That's what a mother's supposed to do isn't it?

When I look at her I feel sick. She's not even trying. She lies in bed, even when he's howling his lungs out. She says she's tired. Tired!

It's been ten weeks. She should be over the birth by now. She's got no idea what tired is. She should try working for that boss of mine. Layin' bricks is no holiday.

Someone's got to keep the money rolling in. Rent's gone up and I owe repayments on the ute. Everything here is hire purchase, even the TV. There's nothin' in the fridge.

So she's got to get the bus? My mother never had a car and never once complained.

She doesn't have to buy baby formulae every week. Just meat and veg, mostly. The trip to the shops is probably the only exercise she gets. Anyway, the ute's mine. I pay the rego.

Find her crying when I get home. "What's wrong with you?" I say. I have to ask her twice before she answers.

"I don't know."

Well I see red. I'd had a shocker of a day at work. One of me mates fell off the scaffold onto a wheelbarrow. I heard the snap of his spine. A crisp snap, like a green branch and there he was, bent backwards like some kind of deformed crab: his arms at odd angles, his eyes open and staring. He was out before the ambulance arrived, thank God. Me boss had to ring his wife. No kids. I could feel my breakfast rising in my throat. Spent my smoko spewin' behind the dunny, so no-one would see.

So there she is cryin' over nothin'. 'Snap out of it!' I yell at her. Then the baby begins screaming. "Look! Look what you've done!" I tell her. "You're useless! Useless!"

I go storming into the nursery and the moment I pick him up I can smell it. Shit.

"You haven't changed him? Can't you see he's filthy? No wonder the bugger is screaming!"

She looks from me to the baby and cries.

"I'm sorry!" she whispers. "I can't..." she begins to

say.

"Can't what?" I shove her against the wall. I don't care that the baby is still in my arms. She doesn't answer.

"Can't what?" I pin her with my elbow. "Can't be bothered to change the baby?" Tears are now streaming down her face. "Can't what?" I spit at her. "Can't pull yourself together?"

The baby is howling now. "Here! Change him!"

She looks at me in alarm and shakes her head.

"Take his effing nappy off and wipe him down!"

"I can't." She doesn't move.

I feel a white anger rise up my body like some kind of a wave. I drag her to the change table and lay the baby down. In a second I have the nappy off. "Here!" I push her head down into the putrid mess. "Here! Your reward for being such a good mother!"

She struggles for a moment and then goes limp. Like a rag doll. She just stands there like some kind of hag. Her face is smeared with shit and her eyes stare back at me. Blank. Like a mannequin in a shop window.

I leave her then. With the baby. I lock her in the room until I calm down and she comes to her senses.

(He looks offstage to signify the nursery. He sits down, rubs hair and picks up an old cup of tea. Pulls face.)

Bloody cold. Can't even manage a decent cup of tea.

(Pause.)

My Dad liked the drink. I won't touch the stuff.

That's what she doesn't get. Loads of men my age wipe themselves out on grog, come home loud and violent.

Not me.

All I ask is a cup of tea and a clean house. Is that too much?

I bloody leave home at six, start work at seven and don't get home until after sunset.

She doesn't know what it is to be tired.

(Pause.)

Mum used to keep a tidy home. Did the best she could with the little bit of money he gave her. Mended our clothes. Mended the furniture when he broke it.

Mended her face when he let fly.

Never went to the doctors. And we never let on at

school. Stoic. That was Mum. Always hoped I'd find someone like her. Thought I had.

Until the baby came.

(Looks in the direction of the nursery. Heads to the edge of the stage and stands as though listening for sound.)

I don't even realise the baby has stopped screaming. I don't know when I notice how quiet it has got. It comes on me slowly, like some horrible understanding.

It takes me a moment to find the key. My fingers just won't work.

(Pause.)

The room is dark. I cross the floor to turn on the night light.

The baby is quiet in his cot. A blanket pulled up

around him.

The room stinks.

The closer I get to the crib the more I can smell it.

(Pauses as though he is deciding whether to continue telling the story.)

She is in the corner.

On the floor.

She's taken the plastic bag from the disposable nappies and put it over her head. She's twisted the end tightly around her neck.

I can't see her face. Her breath has turned the clear plastic opaque. But I can see from where I'm standing she isn't breathing.

There is a pillow on the floor beside the cot. It is smeared with shit.

I think I know then what she's done.

(Long pause. He is staring at the imaginary crib.)

I don't know how long I stand there. Numb. I can't even cry.

I call the ambulance. They call the police.

"What's on her face?" The constable is a woman. She looks at me like I am some kind of criminal.

"Shit."

"How did it come to be there?"

In my mind I see the roughness of my hands on her head, forcing her face into the soiled nappy. I can barely breathe. "She did it to herself. She hasn't been right for months."

"The baby?"

"I thought she'd gone in to change him. I'd just come home from work."

"There was no indication she would do this?"

79

"No."

The police woman narrows her eyes. "Nothing triggered it?"

"No."

She folds her arms. "Have you ever hit your wife?"

"No!"

I see red.

"That's other blokes. Not me!"

(Pause.)

They take a statement. Get the forensics in. Say it's routine. Say it will be hard to keep it out of the papers.

(Long pause.)

The district nurse says she had post natal depression. Says it's not the first case of infanticide by a mother. Says hers was severe.

And the police have backed off.

(Pause.)

I'm relieved.

(Long pause. Looks at his hands. Rubs them as if rubbing out a stain.)

I am not my father.

END

Miss Brown

MISS BROWN alone in a darkened room. A chair and table are spot lit in the centre. There is a glass of water, pills and a camera on the table. She sits on the edge of the light. She has a slight German accent.

MISS BROWN

I said no.

I didn't know who he was when I first met him. He didn't believe me, but it's true. He told me he thought my coyness was charming. That other girls threw themselves at him. That they only wanted one thing. He said he noticed me because I pretended not to notice him.

(Picks up the camera and begins to play with it.)

I wasn't pretending. I had no idea. I'd heard about him and seen his picture in the papers, but people look different in real life.

(She lines up a shot of someone in the audience and takes a photo. Winds the film on.)

When I first looked up from the counter at him I was unimpressed. There stood a short man with dark hair and a moustache which seemed half missing. Skin like bratwurst.

I shook my head when my boss asked me to join them in the studio. "Come and meet Herr Wolff," he said. Herr Hoffman was standing with a group of soldiers who were gathered for their photo. He was gifted. He could make an ordinary man look like a hero when he took their photo.

"Look, Anna!" he never used my first name. He'd hung the portraits in the shop window. "I turn them into gods!" I wondered what magic he would do with Herr Wolff. "Come Anna. Herr Wolff has asked for you. I do not want to disappoint him."

I shook my head and declined politely. There was something about the group of them as they stood huddled together in the studio which made me think of childhood fairy tales. And in the middle of them stood Herr Wolff.

He was not going to take no for an answer. He said that moment of refusal was a challenge. It's what made up his mind he would have me. It's what cemented my future.

(Pause.)

My father kept me pure. Said my innocence would be useful. A difficult thing to do in Weimar Munich.

(She lines up another shot of a different audience member and takes it. Winds the film on slowly, suggestively.)

He sent me to the Catholic school in Munich. No boys allowed. But they were always there waiting by the gates for the bell to ring. Whenever a boy asked to walk me home I had to tell them "No. My father will beat you with a stick!" I knew that later he would beat me with his fist. As my mother learned when she married him.

No boys allowed at the convent business school either. You won't meet men if you're sent to a strict convent in Bavaria!

(She speaks with her father's voice.)

"You will be so different, so pure, so perfect- he will want you."

(Pause.)

I didn't know who 'he' was meant to be, though I imagined my father meant my future husband. I'd been to the movies. I'd read some of the romances my mother kept hidden away. The handsome prince who would slay dragons to rescue the maiden. The brave soldier come back from the war. The hero who conquered his enemies to bring his lady home.

I didn't know it then but the whole country was waiting for a hero. Like my mother and me.

My mother said she'd been mistaken about my father. That his dashing good looks and healthy body covered a darkness inside.
She never said such things when he was home.

(Pause.)

There were things my father didn't know.

(Pause. Lines up another shot. This time of herself. She is looking seriously into the camera. Takes it. Pauses. Slowly winds film on.)

When I was sixteen I loved someone.

Oliver, *(pronounced Oover)* the butcher's son, had taken a liking to me. I would see him whenever my mother and I went to the Marienplatz. Heinrich, the butcher, would smile at my mother and make small talk while Oliver and I would look at each other across the counter. Oliver was a gentle boy. I'd stare at him, at his clear, clean face and his long eyelashes. At his blond hair which seemed always in his eyes. At his smile. And I felt... lighter.

He looked like an angel from the Cathedral window.

We never spoke, but I knew from the blush in his cheeks that he liked me. And when I imagined the heroes and princes in my mother's books I always saw his face.

In the secret place within my heart I wrote his name.

And I hoped my father had saved my innocence for the butcher's son.

(Long pause.)

One day my mother came home with cheeks the colour of ashes and eyes red from crying.

(*Mother's voice.*) "Heinrich's son!" she said. "They killed him! Dragged from the shop into the square as an example."

I could hear her words, but they made no sense to me. Why would anyone harm a hair on that gentle boy's head?

(*Mother's voice.*) "I knew when he didn't join there would be trouble. They won't stand for dissenters! I told Heinrich. I told him there would be trouble. He just said "leave the boy be. He's a good boy. They will see that.""

My mother's words were finding their way into my understanding and I could feel bile rising in my throat. I wanted her to shut her mouth.

(*Mother's voice.*) "Poor Heinrich. He followed them and tried to pull them off, but they held him by the arms. Made him watch. He said the boy never spoke. Never raised his arms to defend himself. Just took punch after punch until he fell over. They kicked him to death."

I pictured his beautiful face. His angel's face. Bloodied and distorted. I closed my eyes to shut it out. But there was no shutting out the knowledge that Oliver was dead.

When my father heard about what they'd done he laughed. "The boy was an idiot," he said. "Only the strong will survive. That butcher's an idiot too if he thinks people don't notice. They notice everything."

Then he turned on my mother. "Fanny, you will not go there any more. You will buy your meat somewhere else."

I saw in my mother's eyes how much she would miss Heinrich. How his kindness was one of the few secret treasures she had to lift her spirits.

He was his father's son. Oliver.

I pitied her. Like me she would obey my father.

(Pause.)

It was not long after this that my father called me

to him and said he had arranged for me to work at Hoffman's studio. "You are lucky. He has promised to teach you if you have any talent. But for now you will be a sales clerk and shop assistant."

I was to dress modestly.

"Take a book," he said.

I thought of the books my mother had hidden away. It hurt to think of them now.

As I stared at him he took one from his desk. "Here. This book." I read the title. *My Struggle.* "You must keep this book with you. You must keep your eyes on its pages. All will be as it must."

I was excited to start work. Hoffman was the best portrait photographer in Munich. He could make people look like movie stars. A part of me wondered whether he could make me look like Lil Dagover. I had seen her film *La Grand Passion* twenty times. There were always people coming and going at Hoffman's. It was a lively place to work. Full of people who were, as he put it, "Full of themselves."

Herr Wolff was a regular. He never came alone. He was always in the company of other men who wore their black uniforms stylishly cut by Hugo Boss; their boots made of expensive leather. Their silver insignia twinkled under Hoffman's lights. I thought how handsome they were. All except Herr Wolff. He was short. He had scraped his hair back over his head and wore a great coat, grey in colour. I smiled when I saw his moustache. Because it seemed ridiculous.

It was then I caught his eye.

And I felt like the girl in the red cloak, lost in the forest.

I blushed and looked down, taking the book from my bag as my father had instructed.

I could feel him staring.

I opened to the first page and pretended to read.

I said 'No!' when the officer came to *invite* me to join them. "You will come." His strong gloved hand claimed my arm and I was *encouraged* in the direction of Herr Wolff who stood smiling behind his grub of a moustache.

I honestly had no idea who he was.

I must have been the only girl in Germany not to know who was standing in Hoffman's studio!

(Puts camera down. Opens purse and takes out lipstick and compact.)

I never finished the book. Lost interest.

(Powders her face.)

My thoughts keep drifting to the books hidden by my mother. Which speak of heroes.

All with blond hair and the faces of angels.

(Opens lipstick and applies it to her lips.)

Germany found her hero and lost her innocence to him.

(Reaches for the pills.)

I lost my innocence too.

Not the day I met Herr Wolff. Nor after.

But before.

I lost my innocence at sixteen.

To the boys in Marienplatz.

(Places capsule delicately between her teeth.

Smiles coldly for the camera as she takes her own

photo.)

And the blood of the butcher's boy.

(Bites on it. For a moment her face registers the

ghastly revelation of the cyanide. The camera

falls.)

LIGHTS OUT

Leviticus

Teenage GIRL. Has blanket wrapped loosely around her shoulders. Speaks defensively at first but as the story unfolds she becomes more open, vulnerable. She is feeling the cold. She pauses and hesitates in the narrative, wraps herself more firmly in the blanket.

GIRL

She wasn't my best friend, or anything. As far as anyone knows. Just a kid from my school. You know, the kind of girl who made way for you in the corridor. Mousy brown hair. Most of them think I hardly noticed her really. I pretended not to.

She had a nice smile. Kind of lit up her face. Kind of made me feel warm inside.

Found her body on the riverbank. They say she hit her head on a branch, that she slipped into the water accidently.

At least that's what the school says happened.

She wasn't the kind of girl to head down there to the river. Not to that spot.

Things happen down by the river.

I've heard the older kids talking and they say... they say she was dead before she hit the water.

It's funny what kids know that adults don't. And it scares me.

She used to sit in my English class. Up the front near the window. Sometimes the light would catch

in her hair and I'd see shimmers of red and gold.
She was good at English. She spoke like she was
from a book herself. One of those adventure
stories where posh English children ride bicycles
and discover treasure. The other kids made fun of
her, but I liked the sound of her voice. I could hear
every part of every word, the music of language
spoken by her mouth. She was always willing to
read, or volunteer. Sometimes, just before Sir
would pick one of us up the back, her hand would
shoot into the air. Like a rescue. Did she know?
Did she know we needed Sir off our backs, that we
didn't know the answers? That we couldn't read
without stumbling and being called idiots?

I'd gone to school with her before.

Before this school.

We went to the Catholic primary school by the

park. They were strict. They went on about God loving us as we were – *Made in God's Image* – and then they'd punish us for being ourselves. I hated it. All they taught me there was that God's got it in for us.

I used to put my electric blanket on high all night, even in summer, so when morning came I'd have a temperature and Mum would let me stay home. I was so miserable she finally took me out of there and I went to the local state school on Smith Street near the Milk Bar. Near the edge of town.

I thought I'd be safer.

There was only one Catholic primary school in our town. One state school. Most of the wealthier kids went to the city to school. Only came back for holidays. Wealthy farmers' kids, not the children of the dirt farmers, wrestling with the scrub. Not the kids of the townies who sold their labour to the farms, like my Dad. Like my brother was destined to do. I was a girl. No-one had any expectations of me. In this town you knew your place. The country's lucky, only for some.

She liked the prayers and the rules more than anyone I know. At least she seemed to. And she was smart. She had this way of asking questions we all wanted the answers to.

 But, as good as she was at learning, she couldn't spell. One day, when I was still in her class at the Catholic school, she couldn't spell the word elephant. We were about seven at the time. There she was, standing at the board with the white board marker in her hands. She was blinking. A grey panic on her face. The teacher waited, telling her *(in a teacher voice)* 'You won't sit down until you spell it correctly!'

'E.L.E.F...'

'No!'

'E.L.L...'

'No!'

'E.L.A...' her voice was becoming a whisper.

'No!'

I realised I was holding my breath.

The longer she stood there, the greyer she became.
Until all she could manage was the E before she
swayed and fell over.

That was what decided me. I had to get out of that
school.

I guess I expected, when it came to high school,
she'd be boarded at one of those big, posh schools
in Sydney. Being so Catholic and all. You know,
the ones with their own tennis courts and

swimming pools. The ones my Dad says the Government steals his taxes for.

But she wasn't.

And there she was, that first day of high school, the only high school in the town, lining up with the other state school kids. And there I was too.

Her uniform was long and her hair was tied back. There was real terror in her eyes. And defiance. Like she was prepared for a fight.

That's where she went wrong.

I was scared too. I'd seen the bigger kids push the Year Sevens off the bus. I'd seen one poor kid struggle out of the junior toilets with his hair all wet and his shirt torn.

I knew if I was to survive the first few months I would have to blend in.

Not stand out.

 Jackals always go after the lone animal. I'd seen
enough David Attenborough to know the ways of
this jungle. My school was full of jackals.
Laughing, shrill, growling. Circling the weak.

They say her mouth was stuffed with paper. One
boy says it was something from a Bible. Not one
page. But a great wad of writing. Leviticus. The
book of rules.

The list of things unclean.

They say her eyes were open.

I picture their sky blue. Clear and bright. Almost
shy, when she smiled.

When she smiled at me.

I don't think I ever felt so warm.

Since they found her I can't stop shaking. Can't seem to warm up. Can't seem to be still. It's like I'm in the river too and the chill has crept into my bones.

No-one knows I was with her that night. No one knows that she was waiting for me, standing outside my window just after ten. When we were supposed to be sleeping. When we were supposed to be in our beds safe under blankets.

But there she was, tapping on my window, like Kathy in Wuthering Heights, but alive. Alive! And she looked so beautiful in the moonlight my breath caught in my throat.

I couldn't do it, you see. I couldn't let the other kids know. They wouldn't understand. There had been two boys at the school when my brother went there. They tried to keep it secret, but someone saw them holding hands at the bottom of the oval. By the end of the day there was a mob waiting. They didn't stand a chance.

She never pushed it. She wasn't ashamed, but she understood my fear. 'It's ok,' she told me. 'We have all the time in the world.'

She sounded so wise. Older, as she held my fingers in her own warm hands. Even now I can feel the softness of her skin. White and smooth. Luminous. Like something from another world.

It wasn't anyone else's business. It was something just for us. A moment when we could forget. A stolen hour when we could be ourselves.

I don't know how she knew I liked her. I pretended the indifference of others. I looked away when she turned in my direction. I avoided sitting near her or being in the same part of the dusty playground. I would steal away to the high grass and the end paddocks where the Ag students kept the sheep.

I was happy to be on my own. I'd sit hidden by the low bushes and watch the sky, looking for clouds, or planes, or birds, anything to hook my imagination onto and fly away. Away from the school, the kids with their hard voices and stares, from my mother who couldn't understand my silences. From my father who may look too hard at his daughter and see something she would rather keep hidden. From my brother and his black-hearted mates. From this town and the dust I felt I was.

What can you say when the language you speak is forbidden?

How do you begin to speak when you are still unsure of what to say?

By what name do you call yourself when the names are stones and your bones are broken?

She seemed thicker skinned. Brave. Strong of heart like the knights in fairy tales. And like the tales told long ago she came in search of her maiden.

"Can I come too?" I blinked at the sound of her voice and looked up to see her standing in the long grass a few feet away. "It just looks like you're escaping." She smiled and I felt my heart stop.

"Whatever."

"Where are you off to, in those daydreams?" she was looking at me now. She was drawing up those long slender legs and sitting beside me. All I could do was shrug. Her eyes danced from my face to the sky above. "Okay. I'll go first. If I could, I would head to the city and lose myself. Go where no-one knows me or expects anything from me. I'd book a flight to anonymity."

I wanted her to think I was clever, so I joked "How will you fill in the form if you can't spell anonymity?"

"Ha!" she laughed. "Thank God for spell check!" then she looked at me, seriously, deeply. "You would be coming with me. So you'd be filling in the form. And spelling properly."

"Me?"

"Sheep see everything, but tell no-one. They are excellent confidants. They don't form mobs with flaming torches. This is the place you feel safe. You are staring at a patch of sky in the same way prisoners do. If you felt like you belonged you wouldn't be looking for escape."

And so began our courtship. Hidden away from the sharp voices and stares. With sheep as our witness. No-one noticed us missing at lunch times. We didn't matter enough.

Some days after school I would go to her house. For an hour. Her mother worked at the local hospital and did afternoon shifts. I'd tell my own mother I was staying later at the library. I'd tell my brother I was on detention. I knew they never talked to each other and I wanted both off my back. Some nights her mother would be home so late she'd be asleep when the front door opened. Her mother always came in to say goodnight. Needed to. There'd been a brother die in his sleep. A baby. Two years before she came into the world. And her mother couldn't bare to change anything in the room, even after she was born. So she began her life in a room painted blue with rockets on the ceiling. "Blue is my feminist manifesto," she told me when I first saw the room. "Nothing speaks emancipation like the colour of the sky!" We'd lie on her floor and imagine ourselves in space. "The ultimate escape."

One afternoon she took my hand as we lay on her floor. Her fingers traced mine like tiny butterflies, mapping the ridges and gullies of my fingerprints. I held my breath. After a few moments she raised herself on one elbow and looked at me. I felt my face roar into flame with the beating of my heart. Slowly she reached out her hand and touched my face. Her fingers were cool and soft and I reached out to hold them, soothing and electrifying on my skin. I wanted to tell her how badly I wanted to touch her, how excited and alive she made me feel, how being with her was like coming home. But I said nothing. I just closed my eyes and soared high above us both into a new world.

She kissed me when she left that last night. From my bedroom window I watched her walk up the path, my heart thudding and my face flushed. Every part of me wanted to pull her back to me, kiss her as she had kissed me.

She turned when she reached the street. The moon was high and her face glowed with such soft light. She was smiling. She raised her hand and traced a heart in the cool night air.

And the world seemed perfect. In that moment. Perfect.

What was she doing by the river?

In the hidden tangle of willow where the older boys take girls from school. Once a girl goes there she's tainted, so they say. They have their own Leviticus, the older boys. They decide the rules. They decide the punishments too.

They are like God. Untouchable.

Yesterday I asked my brother what had happened to those two boys. He shrugged.

In my mind I can see them, smiling at each other. Like she used to smile at me. I can see them touch each other. Tentatively. Gently. Like their fingers are butterflies. I can feel their hearts pounding.

I remember the day he'd come home, blood on the sleeves of his school shirt. There was so much of it I wondered what could possibly bleed that much.

"What did you do?" I asked.

'They were lucky,' he'd laughed. 'The next one

won't be.'

I can't tell anyone where she was that night. They know she sneaked out. She wasn't wearing her pyjamas. She'd put on a t-shirt and a pair of shorts. And runners.

Already the truth of who she was is melting in the acid of their rumours.

And I'm drowning. Drowning in that dirty river, my mouth full of all the things I never told her. There are black stones in my belly dragging me down. Swallowing the blue sky.

She was meeting some boy, so they say.

She was going to that place by the river where the bad girls go.

Bad things happen to girls like that.

"One day," she'd told me. "One day none of this will matter. One day we'll be able to marry each other. One day, when we've escaped, we'll look back on this town and this school and smile. The world is changing. Everything will be all right. You'll see."

LIGHTS OUT

END

Mary
Monologue in three parts

Mary 1

Enter MARY singing/humming a soft melancholic tune, sorting vegetables from a wheelbarrow. Two dark figures (THUGS) enter and stand to the side of the stage. They never speak. They are silently watching. MARY has not seen them, but continues to sort vegetables and hum. After some moments she becomes aware of the audience as the fourth wall.

MARY

Oh. Didn't realise. Don't know where my head is

lately. You know, with all the troubles.

The old woman who lives next door has been closing her shutters when I pass. Have no idea what I've done to her, unless I passed her in the street and didn't realise it.

My husband laughs, "Don't take it all so personally, Mary. You can't make the world happy." Then he kisses me and takes the baby outside to play in the garden.

 And he loves it like his own. Though sometimes I see a sadness in his eyes I wish I had not put there. (*Pause.*) Childhood sweethearts, that's what we were. Our parents were friends. (*Smiles.*) You know the story. But he only had eyes for me and I would never have wanted to look at any other man.

(*Arranges vegetables in bundles, slowly. Pensive.*)

Despite everything, we were meant to be. He's a good man. A prince among men, though you'd never know it to look at him.

He's related to royalty too. His family ruled kingdoms at one point. Lived in palaces. A long way back, so he says. (*Looks at her dirty fingernails and apron. Smiles*) A long, *long* way back. We sure as hell don't live in any palace.

Look at the place! I keep asking him to fix our front door so the lock works and to mend that window over there (*points*), and he says he will, but he does that sort of thing all day long. When he's home he just wants to play with the baby. Men! Are they all giant babies? Food, distraction and sleep. And believe me, the 'distraction' can be exhausting. (*Smiles naughtily.*) Though with him it's mostly fun.

(*Sits on edge of barrow and scrapes dirt from
potatoes.*)

He hasn't been sleeping well lately. He tells me he
wakes for the baby, but I know he's awake long
before we hear any noise from the crib. He thinks I
don't know he's frightened, but I do. I'm scared
too. Something's going on out there. (*Points
beyond the wall.*) Something sinister. Like a
plague. And it's infecting our neighbours, like the
old woman next door.

The family across the road disappeared overnight.
Just a week ago. I was shocked because Mirriam
and I were friends. We'd grown up in the same
town. She had a little boy too. I really looked
forward to our afternoons together, when the boys
were asleep on their rug in the garden and she and
I would share a glass of wine, and laugh, and talk
about the world and our neighbours (*grins

guiltily).

So I didn't understand how she and her whole family could suddenly be gone. Without leaving a word. Without any warning at all.

Next thing I know another family moved in.

I was relieved to see they had small children. I think it's healthy to have my son grow up with other kids. So I decided to bring them a 'welcome to the neighbourhood' gift from my garden. I spent the morning weaving a basket, like my mother had taught me to do. It's an art. And in the old days I know the women of my mother's village would sell them in the market, or make them especially for ceremonies. What better gift than fresh vegetables in a basket woven with love?

I went up to the house and knocked on the door. "Welcome to the neighbourhood!" I said and held out the basket. The man at the door just stood there. Maybe he's deaf, I thought. (*Louder.*) "My name's Mary," I told him, slowly and clearly. "I live over there." Again he just stared.

Behind him, in the darkness, I could see his wife. She shifted on her feet as though the floor on which she stood was a heated skillet and in her arms she held a baby. "Oh!" I said. "You have a baby too. How wonderful! Is it a boy or a girl?" When she realised I was talking to her, the woman frowned and covered over her baby, so I couldn't see it. But the way she looked at me made my blood run cooler in my veins. Maybe it was sick, I thought to myself. Or maybe there was something wrong with it.

My arms were beginning to ache from the weight of the vegetables. I held them up to the man. "Here! I brought you some food. Fresh from my garden. Healthy and tasty and full of goodness." It was then he stepped forward. I thought he was reaching out for the basket and I felt relieved that he finally understood.

Then it all happened so quickly. His huge hand tore the basket from my fingers and threw it onto the street. The basket and all my lovely vegetables were smashed on the dusty road. I was so shocked I didn't even move when I felt his breath on my face. His eyes narrowed on me with a kind of loathing. Suddenly it was clear. I wasn't safe. As I turned to run I heard him spit and felt it hit the back of my head. My feet slipped over the mess of vegetables strewn over the road, but I didn't fall.

I just ran.

Heart pounding, I stumbled into my house. And I cursed my husband when I remembered, the front door had no lock.

LIGHTS DIM

Mary 2

Sad Hebrew music sung/hummed as MARY enters, wheeling a barrow full of vegetables. On top of it is a suitcase. The THUGS enter and become her shadow. MARY does not see them directly but feels their presence. She stops in the middle of the stage and takes the suitcase from the top for the barrow.

MARY

I'm still in shock. Normally my husband laughs everything off.

"Don't get yourself worked up!" He usually says.

"Don't let them get you down, Mary. They're just angry with the world!"

He doesn't say those things any more. He doesn't say much at all. When he and I are alone together we sit in silence. The only time I see him smile is with the baby.

(Opens suitcase and takes out her husband's scarf. Holds it as she speaks.)

I caught him crying in the garden yesterday. Sobbing like he did when he was a boy. He tried to hide it from me. Claims he smashed his thumb with a hammer and that nothing was wrong. But last night it all came out.

(She places the scarf around her neck and becomes her husband. She speaks with her husband's voice. He looks around the stage, touches the walls. As he moves he is shadowed by

I built this place. Me and my father. You watched
us. Daily, after work, we'd clear the land and then
slowly we dug the foundations. Remember those
plans you and I drew when we were twelve? A
simple house. But comfortable. And a garden, big
and thriving for the family we would have. Do you
remember, Mary?

I know every nail and every beam of this place. I
know what is in these walls and what is beneath
our feet. I am a part of this place. It is a part of me.
And I love it, Mary. I love it. And when it was
finished I thought I might die from happiness.

This block, this garden, this soil. It has been in my
family for generations. My grandmother grew
those almond trees over there. Her mother planted

the olives. And the roses I brought you, the day I asked you to marry me, came from the bushes by the door. Roses grew here for as long as anyone can remember.

Oh, Mary, I feel that my blood and my veins and my heart are part of this land. It's not because my family have lived here always. It's because this land is all I am and all I ever want to be.

And I'm afraid. Afraid we can't stay here.

(MARY removes the scarf and speaks as herself.) **As she talks the THUGS begin to search the wheelbarrow.**

Why do we do it? Lie to each other and ourselves? Like him, I pretended that things would get better, that everyone would come to their senses and that our once happy neighbourhood would become safe again.

But it didn't. Those people across the road were the beginning. All around us our friends were going missing. All without warning. And on the street I was stopped and asked questions by the police.

THUGS become physical, begin pushing, touching. They do not speak.

(MARY captures their voices.)

"Where are you going?"

To the market.

"What are you carrying?"

Fruit. What's going on?

"None of your business. Check the basket for weapons."

THUG 1 checks the basket roughly while THUG 2 supervises.

Weapons? Why would you think I was carrying weapons?

"There've been reports. People like you could be hiding anything."

People like me? Hiding? I don't understand.

"Is that a baby in that shawl?"

Yes. My son.

THUG 2 gives order to THUG 1 who obeys.

"Check it. Wouldn't put it past her using the kid to smuggle weapons, or anti-government propaganda."

There must be some mistake. I would never do anything to harm...

"Shut it!"

Day after day the same thing. "Where are you going? You shouldn't be here. Go home!"

And then there were the eggs thrown at the front door. And the rotten meat left on our doorstep – with a sign that said, "Fit for pigs!" One night someone threw a lit branch on the roof, but thankfully it rained.

You bargain with yourself, don't you. You tell yourself that all things pass and that if you can just hold out for long enough then it will all die down. Even when the terrible rumours began to surface and my husband stopped getting work we kept telling ourselves everything would be alright.

Then last night two things happened which broke our resolve: My husband had a nightmare and someone poisoned our garden.

My husband was right. For the sake of our son we had to leave.

———————————————————

Mary 3

MARY is thrown onto the stage by the THUGS who push and drag her throughout her speech.

MARY

My husband said we should tell no-one we were going. We'd heard that they were now arresting people and we didn't want to warn them we were escaping. We carried with us all we could fit in our barrow. We made sure it looked like we were only going to market with our fresh produce.

(She loads the barrow: suitcase first, then hides it under vegetables.)

No-one suspected a thing. But it was hard for him, leaving. And for me. We had no idea if we'd ever be able to come home. We didn't know if our son would ever see the almond trees planted so long ago by his great-grandmother.

We stuck to the back roads. Every now and then we came across others like ourselves. They didn't want to talk. They were frightened. And those who did talk told us stories, terrible stories about what was happening. Stories I didn't want to believe.

It took us days to get to my husband's city. We thought things would be better there. There were many on the road by then. My husband went on ahead to find a place for us to hide, while I waited outside. It was there I met a woman. She was hysterical. She'd torn her clothes and her fingers were bloody from crawling on the stones at the road side. People thought she was mad.

But she was screaming. Over and over again. "They're killing babies! They're killing all the children!"

It was chilling to listen to.

I felt sorry for her. She had to be mad. But she was suffering. So as I waited for my husband I went to her to comfort her and offer her some food. It was then she stopped screaming and looked at me.

She took my arm and said, "They took my son. They are not stopping with him. They want every one of them dead. You must go. Leave here. You must get out!"

"But my husband? I'm waiting for him."

She looked at me with fear. "You must get across the border. You must go now!"

As I looked at her I knew she was telling the truth. So I ran.

I'd heard about a free and safe city across the border in the South. It was a long and dangerous journey. Hundreds of miles. I cried for my husband, not knowing.

I was not prepared.

THUGS rifle through the barrow and find the suitcase.

 I lost most of our possessions on the way. I was stopped many times until I could pay my way through *(vegetables are taken from her)*. And along the way people were both cruel and kind.

It was evening when I finally reached the border. I hammered at the gate calling for help. "Let us in! I screamed. Let us in!"

(She calls but there is no answer.)

"Help us! Help us! Let us in!"

THUGS drag her from the gate and begin to bind her with tape.

(She is struggling to keep hold of her baby.)

"Please! Please! It's not safe here! Please let us in!"

The word Illegal is projected on her body or a screen or both.

"Illegal? How can I be illegal? They're persecuting us, they're killing us, but you call us criminal? I don't understand!"

THUGS gag her mouth. The baby is taken from her.

(She struggles violently.)

SOUND OF BABY SCREAMING

THUG 2 strikes her across the face and she is still.

The image **Illegal** remains projected

until the lights go slowly down.

SOUND OF BABY WAILING AS

LIGHTS GO DOWN SLOWLY

END

Playwright Notes

The monologues in this volume are designed to be performed in intimate venues and classrooms.

All but one (Mary) are completely self contained and require minimum staging. They are adaptable to any environment and can be performed anywhere. That is the purpose of them.

They are particularly suited to both the HSC Drama and English syllabuses (NSW) and are intended to be used in the classroom.

But they are disturbing. They are meant to be unsettling. They are meant to make us think.

I encourage actors to interpret them as they wish and to find their own ways of staging them. For this reason I have kept settings and stage directions to a minimum. Adapt them. Play with them. They are stepping stones to creating something new.

To address the imbalance of opportunities for women in Theatre, most of these pieces are written for women. Most are contemporary, or seem it. One is biographical in nature and designed to give a new perspective on a woman remembered for her infamy (Miss Brown).

Ask yourself if the story of Mary is familiar? Does it resonate in our current political climate?

Would you kill your spouse? If they begged you to end their suffering and preserve their dignity?

Where is Harry? Why won't he come out of his room? And Jimmy Gill? What happened to him?

Performance Rights

Professional Productions:

Feel free to contact me in regard to performance rights for professional productions.

siobhancolman@hotmail.com

Schools

Royalties for certain in-classroom performances may be reduced or waived. No charge will be issued for HSC performance works. Performances at school assemblies do not count as in-classroom performances. Neither do performances at school festivals and competitions. Your eligibility will be assessed automatically when you inquire about or order "Performance rights."

siobhancolman@hotmail.com

My thanks to Donna Dean for her brilliant cover design.

And to Sarah Wiecek for proof reading this edition.

About the Playwright

Siobhan Colman's love of theatre began when she was fifteen and went to see Judy Davis in *Inside The Island* by Louis Nowra. Her journey back to the theatre has been a meandering one. She has been a teacher and a writer. She was convenor of the Women Writers Network of Sydney for over ten years, has been widely published in Australia and USA. In 2008 her play *The Pyramid* was selected for the *30th Anniversary of the Sydney Mardigras* and went on to find audiences in Melbourne and Hobart. She has experience directing and formulating community theatre projects. *Scorpion Tales* is a collection of just some of her monologues.

She is the author of *Pink*.

For more information contact

www.normoyleandcoganpublishers.com